C. D Morgan

Wanderings with the Muses

I0639470

C. D Morgan

Wanderings with the Muses

ISBN/EAN: 9783741186219

Manufactured in Europe, USA, Canada, Australia, Japa

Cover: Foto ©Andreas Hilbeck / pixelio.de

Manufactured and distributed by brebook publishing software
(www.brebook.com)

C. D Morgan

Wanderings with the Muses

WANDERINGS WITH THE MUSES,

OR

FUGITIVE POEMS,

BY

C. D. M.

AUTHOR OF WANDERINGS IN GOWER.

———

SWANSEA:

PRINTED AT THE CAMBRIAN-OFFICE, WIND-STREET.

———

1865.

PREFACE.

THE following Poems, which are the strugglings of an
Infant Muse (being the production of boyhood), are most
humbly laid before the reader. The Author is aware of his
temerity in attempting to climb the heights of Parnassus,
but he trusts that he will be spared the Critic's censure
when the unpretending nature of the little volume is
considered.

POEMS.

SONG OF THE OLD YEAR.

Hush ! hush ! I am dying ; come, mourn for me now,
For the cold hand of death has been passed o'er my brow ;
Let the muffled bells chant a sad knell o'er my grave,
Ere oblivion engulph me beneath its dark wave.

You welcomed me in with fond gladness and mirth,
And happiness circled round many a hearth ;
But onward I sped, like a ghost in the night—
And eyes became dim that once beam'd with delight.

And onward, and onward, and onward I sped ;
And the Peer and the Peasant—I witnessed them dead :
And the maiden that hail'd my bright advent with glee
Lies now in the valley, beneath the yew tree.

And where is the sailor boy, where is he now ?
His form is not seen on the shrouds or the bow ;
Ah, no ! he is lying low down in the deep,
And the storm and the tempest around him they sweep !

And where are the flowers that bloom'd neath my feet,
And the song of fair Summer, that sounded so sweet ?
All gone, all are faded—and I am alone
With the winds of dark midnight and Winter's cold moan.

But I've rattled along, and strange wonders I've seen ;
Over hill, dale, and woodland, and ocean I've been :
On the fierce field of battle I've gazed with affright,
As the mingling of brothers' blood startled my sight.

And I've borne to your ears the dread tidings of war—
The howl of the demons that revelled afar,—
And the cry of the mourner for cherish'd ones slain,
When Moloch's grim chariot swept o'er the red plain.

And I've heard in fair England the weeping for bread,
And seen the pale infant with hunger fall dead !
But I stay'd not nor tarried, but sped on my way,
While death in his vengeance swoop'd down on his prey..

I have seen—but, hush ! there's the sorrowful bell,
I am dying—and slowly they chant my sad knell :
My pulse it grows faint, life is ebbing away—
And thou too must follow, poor atom of clay !

ON SEEING A PRIMROSE IN JANUARY.

Sweet bud of beauty, why art thou
    So soon awaken'd from thy sleep;
Did some soft dew-drop stir thy breast,
    Or round thy heart did sunbeams creep?

Or did some voice from Southern lands
    Breathe music to thy dreamy ear,
And did it sing of gorgeous spring,
    And whisper Flora's form was near?

Alas! frail, hapless, lovely flower,
    Thy syren friends will leave thee die;
No star of hope can beam for thee,
    'In yon dark, scowling, troubled sky.

For now above thy trembling form
    The maddened winds they wildly yell;
And each fierce gust that hurries past
    Bears with it thy sad dying knell.

Death's frosty hand thy life-strings crush,
    The biting hail thy heart will rend;
And cold and draggling rain-drops hard
    Will make thy lovely petals bend.

And so it is with mortal man—
  In life's bright morning all is fair—
But storms and tempests o'er him sweep,
  And friends that flatter'd they are—where?

All gone and vanished, like the dew
  When morning sunbeams robe the sky,—
And pass like shadows from our sight
  When grim misfortune cowers by.

THE FORSAKEN.

Her eyes are weary with weeping now,
There's a clammy hand on her snowy brow,
And back to her bleeding bursting soul
The burning waters of agony roll.

Her cheek is pale, for death is there,
And her heart is writhing in wild despair;
Like a lily crush'd by the savage storm
The maiden was trampled and left forlorn.

She loved,—she fell 'neath her tempter's feet—
For the serpent's poison 'tho deadly, was sweet—
She awoke from her dream, there was sorrow and scorn;
That hour was cursed when the maid was born.

She looked tow'rd Heaven's bright glorious sky,
And the sun in his chariot of gold rolled by;
And she wildly gazed on the streamlet's breast,
And prayed to her God for a place of rest.

And she heard a voice in the springtide breeze,
It played with the zephyrs amid the trees,
And she saw the form of an angel fair,
Who sang of Heaven and the pleasures there.

But she gazed once more on the spangled earth,
On the myriad gems in their beauteous birth;
And joy for a moment beamed in her eye,—
It was sweet to live, it was hard to die.

The scene is changed—she's again a child,
Culling the flowers by the woodland wild;—
And in fancy she roams through the grassy dell,
With the guileless hearts that she loved so well.

The streamlet sings as it sang of yore,
There's the silvered waves on the golden shore,
But a cloud sweeps by with a sombre gloom,
And her soul grows dark as the Stygian tomb.

For she heard the slanderer breathe her name,
She saw them point the finger of shame;
She could bear no more, her spirit fled,
Her heart it broke and—the maid was dead.

THE STONE BREAKER.

When the hail is driving o'er the heath,
  And the wintry winds are keen,
When the clouds are heavy with waters cold,
  A crippled wretch is seen
Cowering low, with shivering limbs,
  On a heap on the blighted moor:
He cannot starve, he must sternly brave
  The storm and the tempests roar.

But the stones are hard and his arms are weak,
  Yet he's toiling there for bread,
For in that hut, where the walls are bare,
  The hungry must be fed:
The man is old and the grave is near—
  He can scarcely crawl or creep—
Yet he's driven out like a worthless dog,
  When the winter snows are deep.

And tho' the night of life has come,
  Yet he's seen on the dreary plain,
With palsied limbs and shrunken frame,
  In the wild and pitiless rain,
Beating the rocks for a hoary crust,
  And wearing his life away—
With none to pity, to shield, or help
  A suffering brother of clay.

And there he sits at his cheerless task,
 ⁻ 'Neath the fierce and fiery sun ;
From the earliest dawn to the twilight dark
   He wearily labours on :
And when sweet spring with her mantle fair
   Is playing amid the trees,
The redbreast in pity seems singing for him,
   As he kneels on his aching knees.

But the bird may pity, the zephyrs may sigh,
   And the flowers may sweetly bloom,
The aching heart will ne'er know rest
   'Till it sleeps in the silent tomb :
O the grave to him will be blissful peace—
   He dreads not that shadowy home,
For his spirit dreams of the Angels' land,
   Where his fetterless soul may roam.

A REVERIE.

The hour was late, I roamed alone
   Beside the withered hedge,—
The wintry waves, with fury wild,
   Dashed o'er the rocky ledge :

The moon her pale cold bosom bared,
  And a million stars shone bright,
But silence, with its dreamy wing
  Seemed hovering o'er the night.

The frost had tried the rich man's door,
  But that was firmly barred,
And then it found the poor man's cot,
  Where hunger's pangs gnawed hard ;

And through the rag-stuffed window-panes
  The stranger groped his way,
And breath'd his biting, stinging breath
  On the shivering worms of clay.

The mother pressed her first-born child
  Close to her famished breast,
The strong man woke, with aching limbs
  And heart that knew not rest—

For famine in that wretched home
  Rose up its gaunt weird head,
And misery wailed its fearful moans,
  And a sombre mantle spread.

I mused a moment, and my thoughts
  Swept on with lightning speed—
I saw the rich in luxury's lap—
  I saw the poor man bleed.

Strange were my thoughts, when suddenly
  A wondrous form drew near,—
Its step was slow, its visage sad,—
  I quailed with awe and fear.

The form passed on, and I beheld,
   Grim misery plume its wing,
And hunger, with a fiendish groan,
   Withdrew its maddening sting.

That form was Death, by Mercy sent,
   And Pity with it came
To rob the poor man's soul of woe,
   And rend life's burning chain.

'Twas done—and Death with sullen brow
   Turned tow'rd the gorgeous hall,
And knelled the rich man's knell aloud,
   And told him he must fall.

How harsh it was ; how hard to die
   And leave the lands and gold !
It must be done—Death touched life's flood
   And froze it icy cold.

But still dark Mammon clutch'd and held
   The life-light of the heart,
And from its home, tho' death was there,
   It could not, would not part.

But soon I saw a phantom bark
   Sweep from the silent shore,
And Mammon's cries were still'd and drown'd
   Amid the water's roar.

The poor man died—his soul was free—
   The rich man died, and where went he ?
I mused on all and gained my door,
   And thank'd my God that made me poor.

THE DISTRESS IN LANCASHIRE.

There's a sore deep cry of agony
    In our sea-embroidered isle;
And eyes are blind with weeping
    That once could sweetly smile.

For the noble sons of labour
    Have been stricken to the earth,
And grim starvation cowers
    Round many a dreary hearth.

But the knell is growling louder,
    And the wound it rankles deep,
And death with unsheathed dagger
    Thro' the lanes and alleys creep.

Like the oak by lightning blighted
    The strong man falleth down,
And the graveyards teem with victims
    In each sorrow-shrouded town.

The bride hath lost the bridegroom,
    Or the bridegroom lost the bride,
The child hath lost its parents,
    Or the parent lost its pride.

Each day, like leaves, they're falling
    To a sad untimely grave :
Stretch forth the hand of pity
    Those tortured souls to save.

Awake up, Christian England !
    Ye lordly in your hall,
Let not hunger o'er your brother
    Spread its deadly, chilly pall :

But give the wealth God gave you
    To shield those in distress ;
And mercy, send thine angel
    Those afflicted ones to bless.

THE OLD MAN'S DREAM.

An old man sat in his lonely room,
    By the faint and flickering fire,
And he heard the knell for the dying year
    Tolled out from the gray church spire.

And he bowed his head on his palsied hands,
    And a tremor thrilled his frame,
But slumber stole o'er the worn old man,
    And a dream of pleasure came.

Away on memory's wings he's borne
    To the far and distant past,
To the sunny days of childhood,
    When the joys were too sweet to last.

He's roaming now o'er the emerald mead,
    He climbs the heathery hill,
And he plays in the laughing happy stream
    By the old quaint village mill.

Another wave of the fairy wand,
    And his youth's sweet joys are seen,
And the fairest spot on memory's page
    Is still in his bosom, green.

For he holds the hand of a gentle girl,
    And rapture thrills his soul,—
But a moment more and his joys are gone,
    And his heart like the ice is cold.

For death has passed in his vengeance by,
    And the lovely flower is slain;
And the old man writhes in bitterest grief,
    And his heart is racked with pain.

This passeth on, and another scene
    Starts up in the old man's view,
'Tis a lonely church with its shadowy yard,
    And a grave by a dark green yew.

'Tis changed once more, and fame is seen
    On a far off hilly crest—
And the dreamer smiles, for his dream is sweet,
    For he fancies he'll be blessed.

And Fame is there with her laurel wreath,
  And her wily whisperings creep
To her lover's ear, to lure him on
  To climb that dizzy steep.

And now upon his furrowed brow
  The knotted veins they start,
And bursting sobs and heaving breast
  Proclaim the throbbing heart.

For Fame is gone with mocking laugh,
  She has robbed him of the crown,
And on the slippery craggy hill,
  Her votarie totters down.

'Twas the last strange phase in the old man's life,
  And with it his spirit fled;
The dream of life was a dream of death,
  For the poor old man lay dead.

THE STRANGER'S DEATH.

Far from his home, from friends afar,
  Weak, worn with age the wanderer came;
He bore with him his little all,
  None asked—none cared to know his name.

One eve the wintry rain fell chill,
  And freezing blasts growled through the vale.
Adown the road with faltering step,
  This stranger wandered worn and pale.

His heaving breast and pallid cheek,
  And leaden film that dimmed his eye,
Told that his woes were near their end,
  That soon from worldly cares he'd fly.

Death's fatal shaft had pierced his heart,
  His failing voice gave forth no cry;
The wild eye told a spirit called,
  He longed to soar above the sky.

They laid him on the stranger's bed,
  They laid the unknown down to die,
How sad, so quiet, the tortured soul,
  No weeping wife, no child was nigh.

He died, he's in the pauper's grave,
  No kinsman knows his last long home,
Around him sculptured marble strewn,
  But Johnston's name bedecks no stone.

The green turf clusters o'er his corse,
  The redbreast warbles o'er his grave,
As soundly sleeps that careworn man,
  As those that riches failed to save.

Near to the churchyard's sombre gloom,
  A little brook glides murmuring by,
And through the yew trees, summer birds
  Are warbling sweet when zephyrs sigh.

The lovely violet sweetly blooms,
  The modest daisy rears its head,
But Johnston sleeps in death's cold tomb,
  Until the grave gives up its dead.

THE FRIENDS OF LONG AGO.

I'm musing, strangely musing, on the merry days that's past,
Of days wove round with sunshine, too fair, too sweet to last,
Dear joyous days, will ye return, a sad voice answers, No !
They're gone, alas, for ever, the days of long ago.

Those days were days of heav'nly mirth, and will remem-
    ber'd be
'Till memory totters on its throne, or death has claimed its fee,
Then friends with faithful hearts were near, but now it is
    not so,
They're gone, alas, for ever, are the friends of long ago.

I dream sometimes of loving ones, and then review the scene,
In visions I'm with youthful friends, or romping on the green,
I ask, are not my manhood's friends as true ? My heart
    says No,
They're not the true dear faithful ones ; the loved of long ago.

Twenty Summer suns are dead, and twenty Winters wild,
Have passed since I the wild flow'rs plucked, a merry-hearted
    child ;
Since then Death, with his bloody feet, have wander'd to .
    and fro,
And green grass clusters o'er the breasts, of Friends of
    Long Ago.

LOVE OF HOME.

O how can the Red Man love the land
   Where the lion makes his den,
Where the deadly cobre lurks secure,
   And the rattlesnake starts in the fen.

Where the air is filled with the dread Simoon,
   And the sands are like molten fire,
Where pestilence reigns and the Upas blooms,
   And death lurks in the rank quagmire.

O how can he love it when danger and death,
   Are ever linked hand in hand,
Why will he not roam where roses bloom
   In the pale man's peaceful land.

Ah! no, he would die in the pale man's land,
   'Mid the gold and the glittering toys,
For his heart would be far in the pathless woods,
   With the hunter's perilous joys.

He could not breathe in the pale man's land,
   Where nature with art is dressed,
For his bosom will yearn and his heart will pant,
   For that hut in the fiery West

There's a magic charm in the pathless woods
    To this hunter fierce and wild,
For he played in the shade of the forest glade,
    When a timid and trembling child.

And he can love as the paleface loves,
    And his thoughts will ever roam,
To the desert land and the burning strand,
    'Tis his wild yet cherished Home.

—

THE EMIGRANT.

—

He left his own dear native vale, the home he loved so well,
His Mother pressed him to her heart; her love no words can
    tell,
He wandered down the old green lane, and past the hawthorn
    tree,
He lingering gazed on hill and dale, for them no more he'd see.

Away he seeks a foreign land, o'er a thousand leagues of foam,
No more across the primrose banks with Ellen will he roam,
He gains the El Dorado shore, one of a daring band,
The streamlet trickles down the hill, rich with the golden
    sand.

A hundred miles from comrades, friends, he's lying all alone
The wind wails o'er the parched up earth, and bears each
    dying moan,
The wild beast, with its bloody fangs, was waiting for its
    prey,
But he dreamt of his distant home, and friends far far away.

His death-dull'd ear, it heeded not, the ravenous wild bird's
    cry,
There's madness in his fiery brain, and wildness in his eye,
He strove to move his full parched lips, but nature was too
    weak,
Yet ere life quits the wasted form, the vulture gluts its beak.

The saddened moon looked sorrowing down, as wolves fought
    for their prey,
And now his bleaching bones are seen, where the wilder'd
    whirlwinds play;
Vain shall his mother weep, and pray that he may safe return,
And vainly Ellen roam at eve down by the limpid burn.

Mother, thy child thou't see no more, nor Ellen be a bride,
A fleshless form is on the heath, where the venom'd reptiles
    hide.
Yet how they longed to hear his voice, to mark his beaming eye,
But storms, alas, sweep o'er the place, where the loved, the
    darling lie.

A woman in a lonely cot, sits in an old arm chair,
Her heaving breast and tear-dimmed eye, tells of her deep
    despair,
Her heart is seared, her grief is sore, list to her ceaseless cry,
"O let me bless my dear lost child, but once before I die."

There is a maid of angel form, but paler than the snow,
She roams down through the grassy dell where the murmuring
    streamlets flow,
It is Ellen, gentle Ellen, she wanders here to weep,
When the village hum is over, and the birds are lulled to sleep.

THE RIFLE VOLUNTEERS.

Through the flow'ry vales of England,
    Let the trumpets' peal be heard,
Blending with the sweet tuned melody,
    Of many a summer bird.
And bear ye whispering zephyrs,
    The stirring notes along,
Through the woodlands o'er the mountains
    Where the skylark trills its song.

It will make the warm blood tingle,
    In the veins of Britain's sons,
For it chants the deeds of olden days,
    Deeds that their sires have done,
And the gentle maids of England,
    Look on with beaming eye,
As they mark the bold hearts ready,
    To protect them or to die.

And o'er Cambria's heathery mountains,
　　Thro' her castles hoar and gray,
O'er the grass-grown camps where Romans,
　　Once battled in their day,
Now is heard wild martial music,
　　And the tread of Cambria's band,
With their mottoes " Death or Liberty,"
　　For the dear old treasur'd land.

But the tramp of Britain's warriors,
　　Does not wake a dread affright,
'Tis but sounding to the listening world
　　That Britons guard their right,
And bold must be the foemen,
　　Tho' their blood-stained swords are bare,
That would beard the dreaded lion,
　　Or would rouse him from his lair.

Around our shores the billows dash,
　　And Britain's Lions brave,
Will show the world that Britons, yet
　　Are rulers of the wave.
And in our heav'n-bless'd island home,
　　We'll banish all our fears,
And cheer with all our heart and strength,
　　For our gallant Volunteers.

ODE TO THE MOON.

Bright beautiful orb, in thy Chariot of light!
I kneel down before thee, beneath the blue sky;
Around thee a myriad of satellites dance,
And dazzle with splendour my wondering eye.

Thou art rolling along in thy tireless course,
As calmly, as brightly as when at the first
Thy Maker he called thee and bade thee go forth,
The black gloomy pinions of darkness to burst.

But what hast thou seen,—ay! what hast thou heard,
Since thy lamp in the heavens with refulgence shone?
Did'st witness the flowers that sprang into life,
To gladden and brighten our terrestial home?

Did'st gaze down on Paradise, lovely and fair,
Did'st witness our parents, pure, guileless, and free;
Did'st feel that cold shudder through heaven that crept,
As the fruit, thrice accursed, was plucked from its tree?

Thou heard'st the wild wailing that filled Heaven's courts,
When myriads of angels wailed an agonized knell;
And thou heard'st the pæans of rejoicings that swept
As the news of man's ruin resounded thro' hell.

Thou heard'st the first cry of the crimson-stained earth,
And myriads, aye, countless, since then thou'st seen slain :
How oft on the battle-field thou hast looked down,
As the mingling of brothers' blood glutted the plain.

Thou wer't list'ning I know, to that whirlwind of groans,
When the waters of vengeance robed mountain and hill,—
And thy light it was guiding the Ark o'er the flood,
When the shrieks of the sinful were silent and still.

When the hosts of Assyria were startled at night,
As the angel passed thro' them, thou marked their dismay:
Kingdoms and nations have crumbled to dust,—
Thou hast seen them like shadows flit strangely away.

Wondrous and wild are the tales thou can'st tell ;
What are the scenes thou art gazing on now ?
Is famine before thee in skeleton form,
Or see'st thou the murderer with blood on his brow ?

Thou art gazing on palaces gorgeous and grand,
Thou art gazing on hovels, the homes of despair ;
Thy rays o'er the gloom of the city is spread,—
But what are the scenes thou art witnessing there ?

Is the oath of profanity borne up to thee,—
Are the deeds of black darkness revealed to thine eye?
Dos't hear the poor friendless ones weeping for bread,
As the proud canting hypocrite passeth them by ?

See'st thou that wretch by the dark river's brink,
Hear'st thou the waters that sullenly roll,—
Satan is there, and the deed it is done,—
But where, tell me where, is the suicide's soul ?

Thou answerest not, thou art fading away,
Yet I know thou wilt rise in thy glory again;
And thou'lt gaze as thou'st done on sorrow and sin,
On bloodshed and murder, oppression and pain.

But e'en to thy splendour there will be an end;
In that wild flood of fire thy glory must lie
'Mid the crashing of worlds, the opening of hell,
With the wreck of creation thou'lt perish and die.

AN EPISODE.

Like a leaf on the roaring torrent,
    Or a ship with rudder lost,—
Like a swimmer deep in the breakers,
    By the world's waves I'm tossed.

But I cried in the fearful tempest
    For a helping arm to save,
Ere the floods of trouble swept me
    To the shade of a gloomy grave.

The rich man's aid I craved it,
    But Mammon grip'd his heart,
And he'd have seen the helpless perish
    Ere he with his gold would part.

But I laughed, tho' my eyes were blinded,
　As the iron gashed my soul,
Yet I would not debase my spirit,
　Not to win the rich man's gold.

For God in his wisdom gave me
　A free and a dauntless mind,
Which showed me the slaves of Mammon
　Besmeared with their loathsome slime.

THE PEASANT CHILD.

You may sing of the joys of a peer or a prince,
　You may sing of the joys of a king,
They will not compare with the peasant child's joys,
　When the butterfly bright is on wing.

The sun's golden pencil paints his cheek brown,
　His hair in the soft breeze is tossed;
Away he is scampering amid the wild flowers
　O'er the mead, when the linnet has crossed.

His laughing is heard in the wild hazel dell
　When the berries are luscious and sweet;
And happy is he 'neath the shady oak tree,
　When his dear little comrades he'll meet.

He plays in the valley, he wades in the rill,
　And he gathers the flow'rets so fair;
His brow is not scar'd, his heart does not ache,
　For he knows not, he dreams not of care.

SILENT TEARS THAT FALL.

There are tears we should dry, there are hearts we should cheer,
    There are souls that are drooping in pain;
There are sisters and brothers now crying to us,—
    But they cry to the heartless in vain.

There are sisters now flaunting the livery of shame,—
    Yet they weep in their agony sore;
Should we not, if we're Christians, the injured ones save,
    And tell them to sorrow no more.

There are children that's weeping—poor orphans are they;
    They're in tears—we should wipe them away:
Should a cloud chill the bud as it bursts into life,
    It may track them through life's gloomy day.

There are friendless ones weeping in sorrow alone,
    And they sink in their sorrows to sleep;
O! how can we stand, if our hearts are not stone,
    And see the poor wretched ones weep?

O should we not try the distressed to relieve,
    Their pains and their sorrows control?
'Twould pluck the sharp pangs from the agonied heart,
    And whisper sweet peace to the soul.

D

LOVE SONG.

I beheld thee, beauteous maiden, fair as angel from above,
And my heart was filled with rapture, with a pure undying love;
Every pulse thrills, quivers, trembles, when thy lovely form
    is nigh,—
O for one sweet smile, my dearest, one soft glance from thy
    bright eye.

Language fails me, when I come to breathe my fervent love
    to thee,
And like an infant, weak I feel,—how can this, can this be ?
I fear a horrid thought, that sweeps like fire across my brain,
I fear, dear maid, thou'lt turn away, and only mock my pain.

Yet could I rend the veil that shrouds my fond and faithful
    heart,
Thou then would'st see thy sovereign power, thy right to
    every part:
Or could I breathe all that I feel, all that my soul would brave,
O then some pity thou woulds't feel for love's unhappy slave.

For fame the poet toils and pants, till brow and cheek turns
    white,
For gold the miser's heart will crave and thirst for day and
    night;
For glory on the soldiers dash, when death is wild and fierce,
Nor heeds the crimson tide that flows, or deadly blades that
    pierce.

So I for thee would strive and toil to make thy life glide on
Like a dream amid the flowers, when winter's winds are gone;
I'd win for thee the miser's gold, and make thy home so
  bright,
Where the birds love-songs should sing to thee, and the rip-
  pling rills delight.

The soldier lured by glory's chains, would not dare more
  than me,
If I could, O my dearest one, but win a smile from thee;
And if I cannot, I will pray for death to close mine eye,
And with blessings for thee on my lips, I'll bless thee and
  I'll die.

THE OLD WELL IN THE VALLEY.

There's an old well in the Valley, where the crystal waters
  spring,
And there the maidens gather, in the sunny eve to sing :
From a hamlet in the highlands would the bonnie lasses trip,
The lily beaming on each brow, the rose upon each lip.

Long, long ere I remember, all our village maids were fair,
But with the upland lasses they never could compare,

And oft-times near that well-side I with joyous heart would
    stray,
When the breeze swept by o'erladen with the od'rous sweets
    of May.

The laughing brooks went singing, thorough the dewy spangled
    glade,
And the wild birds warble sweetly in the woodlands leafy
    shade ;
And twilight came, and Cynthia sailed over the deep blue sky,
When two lovers by the well-side breath'd a fond and wild
    good bye.

By the mossy well they parted, on that fair calm summer
    night,
The peasant boy unfriended, with the weary world must fight,
And the fair and gentle maiden pray'd for him day by day,
Until summer suns had faded and winters rolled away.

But at length o'er dear old England, there swept a fearful tale,
And strong men howled out vengeance, and maiden's cheeks
    grew pale ;
'Twas a tale of fearful battle, and told of thousands slain—
Of a gory hill-side reeking, and a blood-besoddened plain.

Soon, soon, o'er hill and mountain, the dreaded tidings spread,
And mother, wife, and maiden, were mourning loved ones dead,
And onward hastened sorrow to that peaceful little dell,
And like frost upon the lily on the maiden's heart it fell.

Her love was slain, they told her, and her tears they bade
    her dry,
And they whispered of a meeting in the lands beyond the sky :
But in vain they strove to soothe her—for her agony was deep,
And like an infant to its slumber, she sank in death to sleep.

The sunbeams kissed the dewdrops that gemmed the emerald
    spray,
When they found the blighted maiden, but her heart was
    cold as clay ;
She had wandered from her dwelling by the old loved mossy
    well,
Where her trusting heart had uttered, that fond and last
    farewell.

And the village bells pealed sadly, as they laid her in the
    grave,
Where now the snowdrop blossoms and the cypress branches
    wave ;
But by the blazing fireside on winter nights they tell,
Of a fairy spirit haunting the quaint old village well.

LOVE.

Love is the ruling power on earth,
　To which all hearts must bow,
The king upon his gorgeous throne,
　The peasant at his plough.
It sweeps around our wondrous world
　O'er mountain hill and wave,
Its glory brightens childhood's hours,
　And lights us to the grave.

'Tis a star that beams in beauty,
　When there's darkness in the soul,
And its heavenly rays are brightest,
　When sorrows o'er us roll :
In affliction's fiery ordeal,
　On the heart 'twill gladly shine,
And when despair is round us
　'Tis a beacon light divine.

When the world turns coldly from us,
　And we mark the scoffer's sneer,
When our traitor friends have vanished,
　And we weep the bitter tear ;
When the wintry clouds are gathering,
　And all worldly hope seems vain,
Love, like some kind creative power,
　Restores to bliss again.

EVENING.

Wearied and bowed with odorous sweets,
The zephyrs wandered through the vale,
Kissing the violets fair to sleep,
And whisp'ring to the lilies pale.
And far behind the distant hill,
The golden sun stole from the eye,
Yet flung far back his beauteous rays,
As if to say—good bye, good bye.
And far across the azure vault
His glorious purple beams were spread,
And little laughing stars came forth,
And smiled like seraphs o'er my head.
But like to one whose very soul,
Clings to the idol of his heart,
The mellow'd sunbeams firmly cling,
As if 'twere death itself to part.
They seemed to love our spangled earth,
They seemed to love the starry dome;
No wandering exile ever gazed,
More fondly on his fading home.
But twilight closer drew its shade,
And shadows struggled through the dale,
And Cynthia lit her silvery lamp,
In blushing radiance, cold and pale.
The woods were mute, the warblers wild

Had sung the last sweet evening song,
Yet o'er the pebbles crept the brook,
And murmured as it sped along;
It bounded 'neath the hawthorn tree,
Whose snowy branches o'er it bent,
As careless as a guileless child
On wayward sportive play intent.
Methought it had a fairy's voice,
And seemed instilled with joy and life
As little wavelet followed wave,
And mingled in the loving strife:
The flowers drooped their tiny heads,
To drink the pure and crystal dew,
And nodded with the diamond drops,
As silence deep and deeper grew.
How fair and lovely was the scene!
Here echoed no loud strife or din;
Afar from cities and from towns,
With all their surging seas of sin.
I wandered onward through the glen,
And on the " giant's grave " I stood,
Whose spirit, when the tempests howl,
Makes wierdish music in the wood.
What wondrous something can it be,
Which fills our souls with dread affright,
When chance should lead our steps to stray,
Through lonely vales in dead of night?
Pale fear lives in the solemn hush
When nature sinks in sweet repose,

And oft strange terror makes us start,
At e'en the rustling of a rose.
But Oh! I love the twilight hour,
In tangled wood, on craggy peak,
When, from the wondrous spirit land
Strange mystic voices seem to speak.
I love to see the mighty deep,
Sending its singers to the shore;
I love to hear its peaceful hum—
I love its great waves louder roar.
I love to watch Sol's brilliant death,
From some old hoary mountain height,
When like a world of fire he sinks,
And Luna comes to rule the night.
I love, indeed, the Summer eve,
When calmly shines the vesper star,
Then fancy takes its airy flight
To rolling orbs and worlds afar.

SPRING.

An Angel hath come from a far distant shore,
The angry sea knew her, and hushed its fierce roar;
As she stepped on the mountains the heath-bells arose;
As she smiled the sweet violets awoke from repose;
As she breathed on the woodlands the tree-tops were green;
As she whispered the blue-bells and cowslips were seen;
As she passed o'er the moorland, the mead, and the plain,
The meadows grew white with the daisies again.

She came; and O hark! how the mighty woods ring,
Ten thousand glad wild birds are welcoming Spring;
The lark soars away and is lost to the eye,
Proclaiming that Winter, stern Winter must die.
And all things in glory are waking from sleep,
As the sweetest of melody steals o'er the deep.
Then why should the heart of the mourner be sad,
When all God's creation are gleesome and glad?

From the starry mead land, the fair bright land above,
This Angel hath come on her mission of love;
Like a light to the tomb she came breaking the gloom,
And her sweet voice was knelling the storm-spirit's doom;
And loudly there echoed o'er hills and o'er plains
A bursting of fetters and breaking of chains;
And Nature, without e'en a shade of alloy,
Is clapping her fond hands and laughing with joy.

But furious and vengeful the ice-king he fought,
And he killed the sweet flow'rets that Flora had brought;
And he swore on his shield that he never would yield,
As he marshalled his cohorts and sent them afield.
And grimly his banner he flung to the breeze,
And wrote with his diamonds his name on the trees;
And in the lone night when the world turned white,
Away went the north wind to tell of his might.

But vain the proud triumph and vain the proud boast,
The Angel moved onward and hurl'd back the host,
And soon all our mourning and sadness had passed,
And we feared not the tempest, we feared not the blast,
For all were forgotten, all turmoil and strife,
As the words were re-echoed—"awaken to life."
And up, up on high soared the lark to the sky,
To sing the glad chorus that Winter should die.

ON HEARING OF THE FALL OF RICHMOND.

Again there rolls across th' Atlantic's breast
A cry of pain which tells of reeking gore!
And yet again more loud; I would be deaf
And hear no more such horrid tales of strife—

Of fiendish men, athirst for brother's blood,
Alas! proud land, thou'rt wet with tears; thy air
Is filled with wailing sighs, the widow's moan
And orphan's cry resounds o'er all thy hills!
The savage shout of victor, and the shrieks
Of vanquish'd brave ones, are thy music now!
A cloud is o'er thee black as night; no star,
But midnight gloom enwraps thy vengeful shore.
Thy blazing cities and thy sodden'd plains
Should bid thee stay thy fratricidal arm.
Thou'st wearied death, and Moloch sickens sore
At thy intemp'rate rage!   Oh, man! perverse
Thy nature is; for hark! above this din
Of carnage, and the roar of guns and groans
A frenzied shout I hear of battle fierce,
And see thy sons incarnadine the soil.
And this wild, awful dance, no kindred tie
May check.   The sword blade streams; its vengeful
    stroke
Hath sent a brother, or, perchance, a sire
To sleep the sleep of death.   Foul Golgotha
Should be thy name! for thou art cloth'd with skulls,
And rivers wide are surging with thy blood.
How can'st thou gloat on agony?   Will nought
E'en touch thy stony heart?   Art dead to all
To glory and to fame?   Ruin's abroad,
And thou in misery art steep'd.   The dregs
Thou'lt quaff; but ah! 'tis bitter, bitter gall.
In mercy pause: this demon's fury stay:

What can'st thou win, when like a vampire fell,
Thou feed'st upon thyself, work'st thine own fall,
And in thy ruin would'st engulph the world?
'Tis true, thou'rt great and strong, and born of us—
Our child,—we gave thee being, nursed thee, too:
Now thou art free—and thy well-being's ours.
If crimes thou hast, with thee we'd pray to Him,
The God of battle, and the God of peace
To look on thee with love.   Thy ordeal stern
Hath been blood and fire; both have tried thee sore:
Almost too much to bear.—Then quell thy spirit,
And then, perchance, this fearful wrath may cease,
And that command again be heard, as once
'Twas heard of old, when temper'd justice breathed
"Enough enough !—withhold thy murdering hand."

THE STREAMLET.

Where, where hast thou come from, and whither away
Little streamlet—now laughing so happy and gay?
Where, where art thou hastening, and what is the song
Thou art singing so cheerily all the day long?

Thou art splashing and dashing and leaping in glee,
And fondly thou'rt kissing the green willow tree;
Like the humming of fairies re-echoes thy voice,
And the daisies that fringe thee all seem to rejoice.

When gazing thus on thee I feel a strange spell,
And fain would I list to the tale thou can'st tell;
Then softly there came from a starry tipp'd wave
A whisper, saying—like thee I speed to the grave;

To the great mystic ocean that washes each shore
I hasten, and thou mayest see me no more;
But I pause not, I stay not in circle or sweep,
'Till my mother enfolds me and rocks me to sleep.

And as I steal onward I typify thee—
For thou'rt but a wavelet on life's surging sea;
Like me thou must wander and never find rest
'Till thy heart's chords are broken and hushed in thy breast.

For you're all little wavelets—a moment but seen—
The next ye are vanished—none tells ye have been!
Your name and your fame like my bubbles are gone,
As time, in his whirling, rolls dizzily on.

E'en the sunbeams now flooding the sweet Summer sky—
E'en the flow'rets, the fairest and brightest must die:
Then, man! rear not cenotaph, urn, or bust,—
If I am but water: why thou art but dust!

MEMORIES.

Afar from the noisy city, afar from the haunts of men,
There's a dark and tangled woodland, and a green and glassy
glen ;
And there I have oft times wandered in the calm and silent
night,
When the glow-worm's lamp was beaming, and when Cynthia's
brow was bright :
And beneath the waving branches of the oak tree gnarl'd and
old,
Our earliest hopes were plighted, and our earliest love was told.
And we thought o'er life's strange pathway, the flowers of
youth would bloom :—
Ah ! little we dreamt the morrow would come with its
dark'ning gloom.
We little deem'd it a mirage that would vanish and fade from
view,
When the fire of love was burning in our hearts then glad
· and true ;
And we gazed on the crystal streamlet as the moonbeams o'er
it played,
And strove to catch its music as away from the glade it
strayed ;
And we knew that each wavelet's tinkling, that seemed now
like a fairy bell,
Would be lost in the roar of ocean, in the bustling billows' yell!

Yet how sweetly it sang o'er the pebble, where the ring-dove
loves to drink,

And how sweetly it kiss'd the daisy that so lovingly gem'd
its brink.

I whispered, Mary, darling, will the streamlet's faith be thine?

See—see its impatient rushings with the loved of its heart to
twine.

It is leaving the woodbine's odour, and the flower-wreathed
banks so gay,

To curl in the dark blue waters, and leap in the silvery spray.

How it seemeth to mock the fondness of the fair bright
willow tree,—

And can'st thou in thy fondness wander from all in the world
to me,—

Can'st turn from its bright allurings and fly to my heart and
hide,

And in weal, in woe, or in gladness be my own dear gentle
bride?

The maiden's brow flush'd crimson, that was even more fair
than snow,

And her eye, more dark than midnight, now beam'd with a
lustrous glow;

The streamlet, she said, runs laughing to old ocean's breast to
sleep,

And fears neither storm nor tempest that o'er its head will
sweep:

It will live in the deadliest conflict, with the tossing waves
'twill go,

And will share each gleam of sunshine, and be true in each
hour of woe:

'Twill be found in the cold, cold iceberg, 'twill sigh o'er each
    golden strand;
'Twill boil in the troubled cauldron, or sweep round every
    land.
So will I, like the stream, be faithful when sorrows around
    thee fall—
When thou'rt passing life's fiery ordeal, and quaffing its
    bitter gall;
When the friends of thy heart have left thee, and the faith-
    less and false grow cold,—
In thy darkest hour I'll love thee with a love more pure than
    gold !
I pressed her to my fond, fond heart, and kissed her snowy
    brow,
The memory of that blissful hour is hovering round me now
And tho' long years have rolled away, I bless that moonlit
    glade—
For there, beneath pale Cynthia's rays, our deathless vows we
    made.

TO OXFORD.

ON THE REJECTION OF GLADSTONE.

Shame, shame on thee, great seat of learning, shame!
  Why dost thou clutch at mildew and at rust?
Why stain the annals of thy glorious fame,
  When in the vanguard thou should'st stand the first?

Why wilt thou cling to rotten notions old,
  When thou should'st fearless point the onward way?
But ah! thy heart for public weal is cold;
  So, stand thee back, nor bid our progress stay.

Aye back, stand back, and bow thy stubborn head,
  Thou'rt like a nightmare, heavy in the night;
But dreams and nightmares ere the day hath fled
  And fade like dew-drops fore the morning light,

Thy pride hath bound thee with an iron clasp,
  Thine eyes are blinded and refuse to see;
Thus, then, we mock thee as we scorn thy grasp,
  And tell thee freemen yet will dare be free.

Alas! that wisdom should withhold her rays,
  And passion's vile should dare distort her face!
Alas; that she alone refuse to praise,
  And skulks a laggard in the bounding race!

Oh, why dost thou like craven coward hide?
  Why creep like dotard, trembling in the rear?
Awake, rise up, and ope thy portals wide,
  Ere from thy head the golden crown we tear.

Why must I tell thee, when thou know'st full well
  That monks and priestcraft both have had their day;
Anl superstition, too, hath heard its knell,
  And knowledge now exerts its glorious sway.

Then stand not thou an alien in the land—
  Thou hast been dear to every Briton's heart:
In our great work come, give a helping hand,
  And in our labours take a nobler part.

Learn thou, altho' thou hast been born to teach,
  That rank and title, we but deem them vain:
We laud the *toiler* when he strives to reach
  A nation's honour by his mighty brain.

We love the man, who for his country's good,
  Holds up the flag of science to the wind;
Who will not stay where his great grandsire stood,
  But seeks to banish darkness from the mind.

Then if thou'rt faithful, noble, brave, and strong,
  And if thou'dst have us think thee wise and just,
Come forth and battle 'gainst each cruel wrong,
  Nor let us think we have misplaced our trust.

Unlock thy doors and let the hungry in,
   Ask those who thirsteth for fair wisdom's light,
And, if they're worthy, let them honours win,—
   But keep us not in dark, perpetual night.

Fear not: thy fabric will not topple down,
   If thou art founded on the trusty rock;
For greater lustre will adorn thy crown
   If thou wilt yield to innovation's shock.

But if on reeds thou seek'st to lean—beware!
   On moth-worn notions thou must cease to trust,
For if thou dost, altho' thou'rt bright and fair,
   Thou'lt fall down humbled to the humbler dust.

E'en now I see a spectral hand of doom,—
   I hear strange voices round the Nation creep;
Above thy temples there's the wings of gloom,—
   And for thee I could kneel me down and weep.

What hast thou done to cast thy *pearl* away?
   Aloof thou stood'st when thousands sought the prize,
And for a *gem* thou'st taken worthless clay:
   What heavy scales must have encased thine eyes.

See, see, a finger hath enlined the wall!
   The land hath seen it and hath read it well;
Thou would'st not stand and thou art doomed to fall:
   Thou'rt proud and stubborn, so farewell, farewell!

SUGGESTED ON HEARING OF A YOUNG FRIEND ABOUT BEING MARRIED.

Pause, desp'rate youth, and curb love's raging sway,
Nor fling thy long-prized liberty away;
Pause, pause, and on thy reckless folly think,
Ere all too late, thou'rt o'er the fatal brink.
Thou'rt happy now, there's gladness in thine eye,
And from thy bosom ne'er yet came a sigh:
Thy brow is smooth, with not a print of care—
But soon 'twill come, then hark! I cry beware:
Think of the nightly vigils thou must keep,
And "olive branches" that refuse to sleep;
Think, when thou say'st "for better or for worse,"
Of shawls and bonnets, and thy fated purse;
The crinolines in costly show thou'lt see,
Thou'lt pay for all, e'en "nurse" and doctor's fee.
Think of the lectures after all in store,—
Of bills named "legion" and be mad no more;
Think of the ordeal of a washing day,
And of kind friends with whom thou durst not stay;
Think of thy latch-key and thy jolly life,
Of smoky chimneys and a scolding wife;
Think of poor Adam with the traitress Eve,
And Greece, thro' Helen, ruined thou'lt believe;
Think of poor Socrates in days of old,
How vain *his* wisdom to control a scold.
Think, if thou'rt henpecked over life's rough road,
By some man's daughter (chosen for a load),
How sad 'twill be to ever curse thy fate,
And blame the hour that gave to thee a mate.
Think on all this, and if thou'rt noosed and led,
I'll mourn thy fall—but serve thee right to wed.

JUSTIFYING MY ADVICE TO A YOUNG FRIEND ABOUT TO BE MARRIED.

HAVING BEEN CENSURED BY A FRIEND.

My Friend! your strictures are unfair,
　For you to wrong conclusions rush ;
You start when I but cry—beware !
　And warble like a blinded thrush.
Methinks you're like the little mouse,
　Or fabled snail within its shell,
Who thought the Universe his house,
　Wherein nought but himself could dwell.
You know, Sir, you are really blest,
　And fancy all must be the same ;
So fired with zeal and sweetest zest,
　You'd set old Hymen's torch a-flame.
Among the yarns I know of old :
　One story is of tailors three
Who, like yourself, were very bold,
　And for a nation wrote down—WE.
But I look'd o'er the sea of life,
　And heard its wond'rous waters rave,
And marked such fierce connubial strife,
　That, cynic-like, advice I gave.
I saw a pathway washed with tears,
　And heard a sad and mournful knell ;

Of notes, too sad for any ears,—
Sir Cresswell Cresswell knew them well.
'Twas then I rose the "danger" flag,
And bade my heedless friend take heed ;
I hinted life would prove a drag,
If he dashed on with headlong speed.
I told him of his youthful joys,
Of joys that made his heart leap high :
Then spoke of noisy girls and boys,
And warned him how to cast the die.
I meant that he must snap the thread
Of youthful pleasures—single bliss—
That after he had woo'd and wed
He should not pine for that or this.
Yet my experience to my friend
Would say—a married voyage take ;
But what I've said I shall not mend,
I sternly wrote for friendship's sake.
True, I could say that woman's love
By tongue of man might not be told ;
That 'twas a gift from heaven above, —
But scenes around me whispered, hold
It bade me of myself not think,
Tho' I of rapturous bliss could sing
As much as you, although you wink
When I the tocsin loudly ring.
Time flies, and I can only add,
That not fair woman's foe am I ;
In short, they've ever made me glad,

And for them I'd the world defy :
I'd praise them in a melting lay,—
But now must end against my will;
Too much I've said, but yet I'll say—
"With all their faults, I love them still!"

———·

CAMBRIA AND HER PRINCE.

———

Hail! Cambria, dear mother, I bid thee arise
And thy Dragon's red banner fling, fling to the skies,
For thou'rt still the same Cambria, as grand as of yore,
When thy great hills re-echoed Bellona's fierce roar.

And still, like their fathers, thy children are brave ;
They have fought on the desert, they've fought on the wave,
And wherever the flag of old England hath been,
The standard of Cymry the foremost was seen.

Dear Cambria! I love thee, and proudly I'd tell
Of thy heroes, and on thy bright glory I'd dwell ;
I would tear down the veil spun by time in his flight,
And revel in transport and thrilling delight.

I would sing of thy mountains that soar to the sky,
And of groves, dells, and valleys, that gladden the eye;
I would tell how the Celt and the Sassenach oft met,
And how we then conquered—would tell of it yet:

But those ages are gone to their dreamless repose,
And the emblem of Cambria we twine with the rose;
No longer we list to the trumpet's rude blast,
For the hatred of Celt and of Sassenach hath past.

And we've ever been loyal, firm, faithful, and true,
Since Edward cried " Chieftains ! a Man Prince for you !"
And to-day o'er our mountains, to-day o'er our vales,
We're praising, we're blessing the Prince of old Wales.

But alas ! dearest Cambria, a cloud dims thy fame,
For thy Prince we but love him and know him by name,
For he deigns not to come where right welcome he'd be,
To Cambria, old Cambria, the brave and the free.

Then why does he turn from our dear land away,
When our fealty and homage we rev'rently pay;
Why comes he not here as the Prince of our clan ?—
His motto " Ich Dien," hath proclaimed him " our man."

He should have been here when our proudest ones stood
Round the monument reared unto ALBERT THE GOOD,
And of all the earth's nobles no other right hand
Should have bared that fair statue in Cambria's old land.

We give him his title, we honour his sire,
At his nuptials each mountain flung up its red fire,
But he's slighted old Cambria, and scorned her fair vales;
Then why should we honour the Prince of old Wales?

THE OLD LOVED TREE.

'Tis a brave, a noble, dear old tree
    That droops o'er the gushing rill,
And he stands like a sentinel, stern and proud,
    At the foot of the pine-clad hill.

Long years are gone in their trackless flight,
    And I stand 'neath the tree to-day ;
And dreams of a sunny past they come,
    But fade like the wavelet's spray.

I think how I've joyously hastened here
    And sat 'neath the dear old tree,
And the soft, soft moss all around its roots
    Seemed a kingly couch to me.

I think how I've joyously hastened here
    When the weary and worn sought rest;
When the sun had gone, in a flood of fire,
    Away to the far, far west.

And again I look at that silvery flush
    Like a spirit light on the sky,
As the stars they twinkle and whisper of love
    From their wonderful homes on high.

But 'tis past, and I gaze on the dear old tree,
    As memories cross my brain,
And I sigh to think that the hopes of earth
    Like all earthly things, are vain.

THE VOICE OF THE WIND.

I come, the fierce and terrible wind!
  And I'm savagely treading the waves;
And I raise my voice with a mocking shout
  As I open the watery graves.

I come, indeed, from a wondrous land,
  Where man his foot ne'er pressed;
Where the fire-lights dance in the long, long nights
  On the pale snow's glittering breast.

I come—and I laugh with a fiendish laugh,
  As I fling up the starry foam;
As I rush in my wild and my curbless might
  From my strange and my terrible home.

And when I come in a wrathful hour,
  And sweep over land and tide,
That stern and pitiless monster—Death
  Careens by my chariot side.

Then on I dash, in a thundering march,
  And the reddest cheek grows pale,—
But ear hath not heard, nor tongue e'er told
  My strange and my wonderful tale.

In the stygian gloom of the stygian night
  I pass o'er the maddened deep,
And hurl the ship to a markless bed,
  And the brave to a long death sleep.

And the widow may wail and the maiden mourn,
  And the hot tears blind each eye;
But I laugh again as I pile the waves
  On the rocks where the loved ones lie.

MUSINGS.

JOYLESS and gloomy was the darksome day,
For all earth's flow'rs were trodden in the clay;
The storm-lash'd waters leap'd against the shore,
And the caverns echo'd with the troubled roar.
No 'witching music warbled on the breeze,
No zephyrs wander'd 'mid the leafless trees,
No odorous winds went floating sweetly by—
But stygian clouds rushed o'er the sunless sky.

God help the poor man! forc'd to earn his bread
When howling tempests shriek above his head;
When weight of years have bow'd him to the earth,

And nought can cheer him but the hope of death.
O noble is the spirit in the age-torn frame
That nerves to labor—will not stoop to shame :
'Tis not the toiler with his dripping brow,
The stalwart peasant, that I pity now ;
'Tis manhood wreck'd upon the rocks of time—
On a human ruin—I have dar'd to rhyme.

Bleak was the morn, the rain fell chill and cold ;
Snugly ensconc'd those worshippers of gold ;
Around the mansion whirlwinds vainly sweep ;
In gilded parlours no keen breath can creep—
But on the mountain Winter has his throne,
And through the forest storm-fiends wildly groan.
I wander'd onward o'er the steep hill's breast,
Where a son of sorrow knelt him down to rest ;
Life's lamp was flickering in that feeble form,
No bounding current made his sad heart warm—
But shrunken sinews, pains in every limb—
What joy, I wonder'd, had the world for him.
His sunny days were with the things long past,
And now he cower'd in the cutting blast—
But still, no pauper's pittance would he have,
Tho' round him lour'd the shadows of the grave ;
He could not beg: ah, no—he'd sooner die
Than cringe to mighty worms beneath the sky.

Such were my thoughts, when seeing trembling life
So bravely battling in the wintry strife ;

Enduring all his tortur'd frame could stand,
And earning food with weak and palsied hands.

Is this the land, I ask, where Christians dwell,
The home of love, and freedom's home as well?
In this fair land should worthless dogs be fed
When starving brothers ask in vain for bread;
Shall poor humanity give forth its cry
Unheard by all, save him who reigns on high?
Shall wolf-like hunger prowl along its way,
And, 'midst our splendour, boldly seize its prey?
O could we not, by linking heart and hand,
Dispel all sorrow in our glorious land?
Could we not soothe the poor man's rugged road,
Could we not pluck from famine that sharp goad;
Could we not whisper peace to those distress'd,
And bid the troubled waters be at rest?
Yes, yes, if man would truly love his kind,
No more earth's griefs and sorrows should we find;
But pure felicity would brightly shine,
And earth, indeed, would be a world divine.

THE MUSIC I LOVE.

I love the sweet music of harp or of lyre,
　　When wakened to life by the finger of clay ;
I love the loud anthem, to heaven ascending,
　　Or a peasant girl trilling some sorrowful lay.

But, Oh ! 'tis the music of nature I worship—
　　The sigh of the zephyr, that stirs the green tree,
The song of the streamlet, like fairy bells tinkling,—
　　E'en the breeze o'er the mountain has music for me.

I listen entranced, when the sun-lighted billows
　　Are chanting strange melodies o'er the bright sand,
As wavelet on wavelet rolls, swelling the chorus,
　　I deem it sweet music from some mystic land.

But dearer than all is the voice of the tempest,
　　The hurricane howling o'er moorland and plain—
When the winds of dark midnight are shrieking like furies,
　　And lone woods are writhing and groaning in pain.

How grand and sublime is the loud thunder's pealing,
　　That shakes the firm earth, and e'en startles the sky
With the hiss of the fire-flash on the blast riding ;
　　And, blending with all, comes the storm-spirit's cry.

When the great waves are roused from a long dream in anger,
　　And leap like mad demons against the black shore,
How wondrous the war-notes, now louder and louder,
　　The wild waters drowning the hoarse thunder's roar.

The wail of the whirlwind, the boom of the surges,
  The shout of the sea-king in wrath on the deep ;
The rush of the torrents that bounds through the valley,—
  What chords there are struck in the cataract's leap.

Then Nature, 'tis thine is the music for me,
  And with thee I'd join thy Creator to praise ;
To Him who hath taught winds and waters to sing
  My voice to His glory and goodness I'll raise.

———

SPRING FLOWERS.

———

PRELUDE TO SUMMER FLOWERS.

———

Ye are gone, my bright and beautiful—
Ye are gone to your graves to sleep ;
And tho' sunbeams play around ye,
I could kneel o'er your graves and weep.

Ye came when the earth was sorrowing,—
Ye came just one by one,
And heard the wild birds warble ;—
But now, alas ! you're gone.

The hills were bleak and barren,
Not a leaflet gemmed a tree,—
But the snow-drop op'ed its bosom,
And bade stern Winter flee.

The braes were cold and cheerless
When the violet reared its head,
And o'er it perched the redbreast,
And sang for Winter dead.

The wild wood sounded hollow,
When the bright anemones came ;
But they are gone with the many,—
Gone like the breath of fame.

The streamlet murmured sadly,
When the primrose fair awoke ;
But soon it leaped to music,
For it knew its chains were broke.

Grey were the meads and blighted
When the golden cowslip rose ;
But the green blades gathered round it
When its brilliant eyes would close.

So, like the flowers of spring-time,
We all must pass away ;
How fleet is our little moments,
How frail is the breath in clay.

But again will the flow'rets blossom,
When the wintry days are passed :
And we shall start from slumber
At that long loud trumpet's blast.

But now ye are gone my beautiful,
Ye are gone to your graves to sleep,
And tho' sunbeams dance around ye,
I would kneel o'er your graves to weep.

ON THE DEATH OF A FRIEND.

They have borne death's noble victim to the churchyard*
    'neath the hill,
And a faithful heart is silent and a tuneful tongue is still:
In the springtide of his manhood he was swallowed by the
    tomb,
O'er the sunshine of life's beauty death has cast a sombre
    gloom.

And there, amid the young and aged, they have laid him
    down to sleep,
Where the pale sad moon is gazing, and the stars of midnight
    weep;
And to his solemn resting place our aching hearts will turn—
For a friend so loved and valued we can never cease to mourn.
                    *Reynoldstone.

O sterling were his virtues and brilliant was his mind ;
Alas ! in earth's wild wilderness how few like him we find—
For none could be his enemy—he was so good, so mild,
With heart that knew not malice, and as guileless as a child.

Hard, hard he strove for knowledge, and he woo'd her
    beauty bright,—
But in poor benighted Gowerland they've hid her glorious
    light ;
And ghost-like voices echo from the peasant's humble graves—
From those whose minds were darkened, and who lived and
    died like slaves.

But alas ! futile were his studies, all his dreams and hopes
    were vain,—
No earthly tie could bind him to this weary world of pain ;
And, altho' we fondly loved him, we shall never see him more
'Till we cross death's broad wide ocean, and gain that
    wondrous shore.

LIFE.

SUGGESTED BY HEARING MR. T. COOPER LECTURE ON FUTURITY.

———

O Life! thou art a strange mysterious thing!
Where dost thou wander on thy flashing wing?
When death unyokes thee from thy clayey load,
Where dost thou soar to on thy pathless road?
Hast thou a dwelling in yon azure sky,
Above that star which beams before mine eye?
I strain my vision, and I strive to peer
Beyond the confines of this mighty sphere.
I fain thro' vast immensity would gaze,
Where neither star nor meteor's fire can blaze:
I span in thought the utmost bounds of space—
But fancy cannot reach thy resting place.
Ethereal essence of the great first cause,
Obeying none but *His*, Jehovah's laws:
I feel thee working in each leaping vein—
O'er all creation thou dost proudly reign—
The heather blooming on the lofty hill,
The daisy blushing by the tinkling rill,—
All moving things that wander o'er the earth—
The beasts "that perish," they have vital breath.
But ah! 'tis man, 'tis mighty man alone
Who claims a title to a glorious throne
'Tis man, who flits here but a little day,
Who'll live when all things shall have passed away.
Then sceptics breathe not your destroying creed,

Your hearts' loud teachings 'twould be well to heed :
Will pre-monitions not engender fear,
And tell you that your wondrous home's not here ?
We pace the graveyard, view the chisel'd stones,
Where crumbling dust falls from the mould'ring bones ;
The spark that wandered through the mighty brain,
Can that with ruin and the worms remain ?
Can thought and reason with corruption sleep
In dark oblivion, in her chambers deep
Beneath the sod, till time shall cease to roll—
Can death consign a never-dying soul ?
Ah no ! the lyre, the frail material clay
Is all that will, is all that can decay.
Then throb on heart, for far beyond the tomb
There is a land with neither shade nor gloom.

————

THE   GHOST.

————

One night in musing mood I sat
Within my lonely cot :
There, dreaming o'er the shadowy past,
O, could it be forgot !

To drive the gloomy thoughts away
I wandered from my room,
For all alone the silence seemed
The silence of the tomb.
I gazed upon the placid sky,
With myriad sapphires bright,
As Luna flooded all the heavens
In lustrous silvery light.
With careless steps I onward went,
And passed each haunted nook
Where peasant boys oft scamper by,
Too frighten'd e'en to look.
At length I left the rugged road
And crossed the frosted field,
Some power seem'd o'er me, and, tho' loath,
I nought could do but yield.
How silent !—not a sound I heard
Save yonder hooting owl,
And nearer and yet nearer still
The house-dog's hideous howl :
The cock, too, perched beside the way,
Now crowed both loud and shrill ;
It had seen, no doubt, some sable train
Slow wending up the hill.
For they can see strange candles walk
And coffins borne along,
When man cannot (or very few)
Perceive the spectral throng.
Unheeding where my steps would lead—

The field I paced it o'er,
And saw before my eyes a sight
Which ne'er was seen before.
Transfix'd with terror there I stood,
Cold sweat ran o'er my brow :
The mem'ry of that fearful scene
E'en makes me tremble now.
I could not move, and knee smote knee—
My teeth beat in my head ;
And though I ten times tried to speak
I could not,—speech had fled.
O horror! 'twas a ghastly form,
Huge, fleshless, gaunt, and black :
Its eyes seem'd rolling balls of fire,
And wings were on its back.
Closer the hideous object came,
And motion'd me to speak ;
I knew its wish, it was that I
Should first the silence break.
I tried, and said, I know thee not—
As upright stood each hair ;
Not know me ? list ! I am the Ghost
Of Old Will Griffith's Mare !
I know thee well, aye, very well,
Thou lead'st a lonely life,
And tho' thou'rt trying very oft
Thou can'st not get a wife :
I've pulled the coals to keep thee warm,
Toiled, strained up many a hill,

And then stood starving by thy door
When thou wert feeding Will.
One night—O how I cursed ye both !
For furious fell the rain,
And one great sore upon my back,
It made me groan with pain :
And with an hungry belly too,
Tied by thy door to stay,
'Till Will had had his brimming glass
And pocketed his pay.
But never mind—'tis past and o'er,
And harm thee now I'll not—
I only wish to let thee know
That 'tis not all forgot.
So don't stand shaking shivering there,
Though thou'st not pitied me
I'll show thee I no malice bear,
For I will pity thee.
This is the solemn midnight hour
When ghosts and goblins walk ;
I've met thee in this solemn time,
And with thee I must talk.
To thee a tale I will relate—
'Twill make thee really stare ;
And thou must tell to brutes and men
The fate of Will's old mare.
I very lately was on earth
In flesh, or rather bones ;
Thou cam'st to see me ere I died

And heard'st my piteous groans.
I lost my strength when winter came,
For I'd no place to feed,
I tried to eat the prickly furze—
I picked each straggling weed.
But soon I nothing had to eat,
And then I weaker grew—
And, swearing that I could'nt work,
Old Will his knife he drew.
He plunged it in my scraggy neck —
Scarce any blood was there ;
But out the little tide it came,
And so died Griffiths' mare.
Now when the knife leaped in my throat
(For a murder'd mare am I),
My spirit left, and to the land
Of spirits thought to fly.
I did, and saw a wond'rous place
Where lovely grass bloom'd green,
And cooling winds went sighing on,
And silvery streams were seen.
No gnats, no brims would sting me there—
No whipping no " gee wo ;"
I asked the ferryman to cross—
He grimly answered : No,
Between thee and yon happy land
This river broad must sweep,
For thou art doomed this side to stay
To gnash thy teeth, and weep.

I

I gazed with rapture at the shore,
And saw each beauteous glade ;
I marked a myriad steeds at play
Beneath the glorious shade.
And far as e'er the eye could reach
There lay a flow'ry plain,
Where sleek fat coursers bounded on
Unchecked by bit or rein.
I saw them drinking in the rills
O'er which the sunbeams played,
And through the grass, which reached their backs,
In sportive glee they strayed.
Methought there is no Winter there—
No pulling coals I thought :
No Wills to spend each penny piece
Which sweating nags had got.
O with what wild delight I neighed,
And rushed the tide to dare,
But ere I leaped a voice cried " Back !
Stand back Will Griffiths' mare ! "
I saw the monster raise a whip—
'Twas barbed with serpents' darts :
" Begone," he said, " this thong I use
To scourge all erring hearts.
And thou art stained with many crimes,
So thou'lt not enter there ;
I'm ordered not to let thee pass,
So stand back, Griffiths' mare."
I said, your're very cruel, Sir,

Think on my earthly pain,
I'm sure I've suffered quite enough
To purchase yon domain.
" We'll see," he said, then loud he called,
And forth two spirits came—
" Bring me the records here at once,
And find this creature's name."
Two books they brought, and one, I saw,
Was written o'er and o'er ;
He shook his head and looked at me,
Saying " No, thou'lt not go o'er."
I marked his brow grow stiff and stern,
And deadly turned his eye,
I trembled like an aspen leaf,
And gave a plaintive cry.
My crimes, I said, are very great,
Aye, more than I can bear ;
But all those sins were done when I
Was old Will Griffiths' mare.
" That's true," he said, " but in this book,
Here in this journal's kept
Account of every ravaged field,
Of every hedge you've leapt.
For years you've led a wicked life,
Broke hedges, trampled grass ;
So, scourged and fettered, you'll be sent
Where torments may not pass.
Bring forth the chains —and at his word
A grisly spirit brought

A mass of fetters, and each link
Was from the furnace hot.
"Behold," he said, "yon desert land,
Where pain and endless night
Reigns ever there—that is thy doom
Away; now leave my sight."
They forced me on, but lo! their king,
By chance he came that way,
He bade the monsters loose my chains,
And flung them far away.
"I know," he said, and turned to me,
"Thou'rt well acquaint with care,"—
Who art I bowed, great king I cried,
I'm old Will Griffith's mare.
I've left my bones upon a bank
For dogs to rip and tear:
They've even stripped my poor old hide,
And sold my tail for hair.
Of worldly cares you know, great king,
I've had a moustrous share,
And now, I think they're very hard
On old Will Griffiths' mare.
He said—"Thou'st led a wicked life,
In short, a life of sin—
And thou can'st not approach those fields
'Till penance gets thee in:
In purgatory thou must stay,
And try to purge off there
The sins committed, while on earth,

By thee, Will Griffiths' mare.
I'll take some pity on thy case—
As hunger was the cause—
But cannot dare forgive thee now,
For just are all our laws;
But thou shalt some day tread yon fields,"
And then he turned away,
And, freed from fetters, I am left
Where many horses stray.
I've power to roam at midnight dark—
To stop me none may dare;
And thou must others warn by me,
By me! Will Griffiths' mare.
Thou'lt learn our tongue, our secret tongue,
How horses do converse,
And then my story thou can'st tell—
My sufferings rehearse.
I'll teach thee when we meet again,
For now I cannot stay;
I'll just prepare thee for the work
Thou'lt do another day.
Thou'lt tell the horse that Will has now—
That's doing all his work,
Whilst Will is going on the same:
As savage as a Turk.
That if he ever sees a ' shord,'
He'd better not go in,
Or happy quarters when he dies,
Tell him he'll never win.

I know he'll feel it very hard,
To keep this stringent law,
When hunger's pangs will urge him on
By grating at his maw.
But better far to suffer here
Where life'is scarce a day,
Than he should come to where I am,
Where time ne'er fades away.
And tell, again, thy brother man,
They'd better all take heed ;
Warn all those money-loving grubs,
Whose very souls are greed.
Tell them that every secret act
Is in a ledger writ—
Not one foul thought or base design
Does our great Clerk omit.
And when accounts are balanced up
Right sadly will they fare ;
If they do not (now they have time)
Attempt to make things square.
And if thou see'st th'oppressors' hand
Pressed heavy on the weak—
Don't shield the monster in his work,
But bold and fearless speak.
Tell the rich tyrant there's a day
When big and small must stand,
To prove their titles (clear as light)
To yonder glorious land.
And if they're rolling here in gold,

'Tis sent to them to use ;
And woe befal them if they should
God's favor dare abuse.
Tell them they've not been given wealth
To crush the poor man down—
To make him stand, with hat in hand,
Pale trembling at their frown.
Tell them their deeds they cannot hide
From Him who rules on high,
Who listens to the widow's wail,
The orphan's piteous cry.
Tell them—ah hush ! I must be gone,
I've overstepp'd my time
I've more to say, which thou must put
Some other day in rhyme.
So now farewell, till next we meet,
Mind of thyself take care—
Come, say good bye !—of course, 1 said
"Good bye, Will Griffith's Mare."

———

SONG OF WINTER.

———

Hurrah ! I am king ! I am king o'er the earth,
My banner floats wildered and free,
I ve withered the flowers, they're blighted and dead,
And I've roused up the fiends of the sea.

When my coursers were pawing afar in the North,
   Their neighing was borne on the wind,
At that sound the green leaves donned the liv'ry of death,
   And the songsters were sadden'd and still'd.

Then I marched o'er the deep, and the mad spirits danced,
   And dash'd the wild waves to the sky,
Whilst howlings and wailings from monsters so fierce,
   Swept furious and hurriedly by.

I'ue mantled the earth and I've fettered the brook,
   I've torn up the valley and dell,
I've shivered the forest—the kings of the wood
   'Neath my fury they helplessly fell.

A SUMMER STORM.

There's dark clouds descending o'er yonder high hill,
   Way down in the woodlands the songsters are still;
The branches are tossing as the wild breeze comes on,
   The thunder is roaring and the sunlight is gone.

The violet shudders in its green mossy bed;
   The daisies are drooping and fall as if dead,
The birds spread their wings o'er their frail little nests,
   And press their lov'd little ones close to their breasts.

Hark! up comes the storm, see the wild king is free,
  And the fierce storm is raging out out o'er the sea;
Through the valley it echoes—the forests are rent
  And the stalks of the flowers are broken and bent.

It has passed in its fury, but its footprints were death,
  And the rose and the lily lie crushed on the earth;
But each wood-bird is warbling its sweet little song,
  They've forgotten the storm-king who tarried not long.

A DOG'S APPEAL.

I had a friend in sorrow's hour,
Faithful and true in storm and shower,
To make him false none had the power
    His heart was kind;—
A nobler, e'en in the human race,
    Ye ne'er could find.

But fate's stern mandate bade us part,
And "Bob," he almost broke his heart,
He cried, he whin'd with leap and start;
    For he'd been told
That he that day had basely been
    Disclaimed—Disowned.

J

But look'd at me, tears dimmed his eye,
And said, alas! I'm doomed to die,
Quoth I, who said so told a lie,
  I'll set thee free,
And those who're thirsting for thy life,
  Must come to me.

But, ah! said "Bob," you're very poor,
I've seen the wolf grin by your door,
'Tis true he ne'er has trod your floor,
  Yet you must fight
To keep him off you're bound to toil,
  With all your might.

So I would rather now be shot,
Than you should give that bloated lot,
For my poor sake one single groat,
  The ravenous crew,
Who press the poor with iron heel,
  And trample you.

But yet, quoth "Bob," it has been said,
By sages who were deeply read,
That freedom o'er our land is spread,
  Yet here must I,
Twelve shillings pay to tyrant knaves,
  Or else must die.

I think it is a monstrous shame,
The legislature is to blame,
And to the Chancellor—what's his name—
  I wish you'd write;
But, as you're hasty in your moods—
  Mind be polite.

Just tell him I'm a thorough dog,
No crawling, servile, ugly frog;
That I've no pockets made for prog,
  Say I am true,
Not like those horse-leech sycophants,
  That cringe round you.

And ask him why they pounce on me,
When puppies walk on two legs free,
And some before them bow the knee,
  Yet I must pay
To breathe the air in freedom's home,
  Or skulk away.

And say 'tis not a Christian thing,
To hang me up with greasy string,
Or drown me with a savage fling,
  'Twould murder be,
And when the oppressed the oppressor meets
  They'll hear of me.

" Bob's" tongue grew mute, he drooped his ears,
And down his face ran scalding tears;
But when I said I'd pay th'arrears,
  He barked with glee,
My word I'll keep—knaves, take my purse,
  " Bob " shall be free.

THE LAST DAYS OF AUTUMN.

How sad and silent are the woodlands dark,
No more up heav'nward soars the joyous lark,
Strange winds are wand'ring thro' the trembling trees,
And stricken leaflets flutter on the breeze;
Hush'd are the songsters, and the cooing dove
Hails not the sunbeams with its song of love,
But solemn awe hangs heavy over all,
As death stalks onward with its blighting pall;
The heather blooms not on the mountain height,
And faint and weaker grows Aurora's light,
The streamlet growls upon its pebbly bed,
It kiss'd the lily, but the flower was dead.
Hark how the caverns echo with the roar
Of angry waters wrestling on the shore!
And o'er the great and ever flowing deep,
The tempests gather and the whirlwinds sweep;
Yet how sublime and glorious is the scene,
A cloud of gold o'er all the woods are seen,
And as the sunbeams flood the fair blue sky,
A flush of beauty greets the won'dring eye!
It seems as Nature ere she sinks to rest,
In all her robes of lov'liness is dress'd;
But, 'midst the splendour there's a sombre gloom,
The fairest flowers have found a silent tomb;
This gorgeous grandeur, born of chill decay,

Like fairy visions soon must fade away;
Yet what a lesson is it man to thee,
Behold the glory of that golden tree.
It blush'd in gladness in the merry spring,
Its branches rustled with the zephyr's wing;
The genial Summer blessed it as it passed,
But now its knell is knolled upon the blast.
So all things perish in one little day,
The fairest, brightest—all must pass away.

SONG OF THE NEW YEAR.

I come on the wings of the wandering winds,
   On the lightning's crest I ride;
And I sweep along o'er the wondering world,
   Where the storm and the tempest hide.

My fiery steeds, they madly bound
   And rush like the whirlwind on:
You ope your eyes in the happy New Year,
   You close them, and ah! I am gone.

I flit away like the meteor's flash,
   Or a dream in a Summer's night;
And man cannot bridle my mighty power,
   Though I boldly challenge his might.

I only laugh, and o'er the deep
  The waves in mountains swell ;
And I fling my wand o'er the startled land,
  And the storm-fiends wildly yell.

And I spread a shroud of shivering death
  O'er mountain, vale, and hill ;
And I breathe, and lo ! the laughing brook
  In icy chains is still.

And again I march through the forest dark,
  And shriek till the woodlands groan ;
And the oak of a thousand years lie rent—
  While the hollow caverns moan.

Sorrow and joy, love, peace, and death
  I bear in my arms along ;—
You will hear the wail for the mighty slain—
  And you'll hear the nuptial song.

But nought to me is the song of joy,
  For I speed along on my way ;
And the world may jog as it did of old,
  Or be as it is to-day.

"THE CLIMATE OF ENGLAND."

SUGGESTED BY HEARING OF A PERSON AS AUTHOR OF THE

"CLIMATE."

We've really borne this long enough,
   We cannot, will not, stand it more ;
We'll send the weather's author off
   To some wild, sterile, hideous shore.

We'll put him in our swiftest ship,
   And bid the howling winds creep on,
And give three lusty, heartfelt cheers
   To know our fierce disturber's gone.

We'll fling him on some gloomy land,
   Where arid deserts meet the eye ;
Where ne'er a flow'ret dares to bloom,
   And nought but tempests fill the sky.

And there we'll leave him, all alone,
   Like Selkirk, steep'd in solitude ;
Unhoused, uncovered, let him feel
   The storms his mystic arts have brew'd,

I don't know what we've done to him,
   To rouse his wrath and savage ire—
Unless 'tis that the climate failed
   To reach the author's own desire.

And what he meant, I cannot think,
 To bid the rain like torrents fall;
Upon my word I fear'd he meant
 To drown us Welshmen one and all.

He drove the sunlight from the sky,
 And made the poor old moon turn white;
The stars their little faces hid,
 And almost turned our day to night.

He roused old Boreas from his sleep,
 And tossed and tumbled Neptune's bed;
He loosed the spirits of the storm,
 And o'er our land their pinions spread.

He changed the music of our rills,
 And made them leap and loudly roar;
He hushed the warblers of our groves,
 And bade them never cheer us more.

He robbed as of our sunny eves,
 He spoiled the lovers' moonlight walk;
He shook old Atlas and his load—
 At least such was the common talk.

He sent his lightnings through the woods,
 And stretched the oak tree on the earth;
He spread his waters o'er the plain,
 And nature groan'd in sombre dearth.

He'd often prophesy and tell
    Of coming tempests, winds, and rain ;
It was a shame to hoax us so,
    And fright us o'er and o'er again.

Indeed, there's been a horrid change,
    We once could call our climate fine ;—
We had the cheerful wint'ry frost,
    And summer suns did brightly shine.

We had no 'taters' rotting then ;
    Our sheep and cattle all did thrive :
But now, the doctor's greatest skill
    Can't keep our flocks and herds alive.

But we must stop this Author's fun,
    And send him far enough away
To where the Gnomes and Furies dwell,
    And there for ever let him stay.

But, should he 'scape his jailor's charge,
    And, mounting with the whirlwind's king,
Return again to Britain's isle,
    Then on his head our rage he'll bring :

For in our land he shall not lurk ;
    We'll pull him from each hiding place,
And tie him to a comet's tail,
    We'll send him whirling into space.

K

ON THE WELCOME APPEARANCE OF FINE WEATHER.

"THE CLIMATE OF ENGLAND."—ITS AUTHOR.

Kind friends a moment's favour, I have a loud demand,
For I claim the thanks and gratitude of all in Cambria's land ;
I'm sure you all remember, for your mem'ry cannot fail,
Of my threat to tie an Author fast to a comet's tail :
And I said I'd send him whirling thro' vast and boundless
    space,
And that in storm-toss'd England he should have no dwelling
    place ;
Or on some arid desert I said he should be cast,
Where the spirits of the tempest ever ride upon the blast.

I said to and I meant it, and that well the Author knew,
For he soon called home the hurricanes which fiercely round
    us blew,
He swept aside the cloud-flakes and Sol broke forth so bright,
And bathed the craggy mountain-tops in floods of golden light.
And Spring came all in glory, unfettered, fair, and free,
And wild birds warbled merrily from every blushing tree ;
But still, amid this gladness, there came a chilling tale,
And the ploughman's hand grew nerveless, and his honest
    face grew pale.

For the " Climate's" Author told us that our fertile fields
    would fail—
We should hear no song of harvest nor sound of threshers'
    flail ;
We should not, he said, in seed time dare furrow Mother Earth,
But all the land would tremble 'neath a chill and freezing
    dearth.
And he bade us all be chary, and husband well our store,
For he said he felt quite certain we should ne'er have any more,
And many things he told us which filled our hearts with
    dread—
But I, alas! was faithless, and laughed at all he said.

For I thought perhaps the " prophet " might be of that
    strange race, ;
Who claimed " Eli " for a father in that now degraded place ;
So I said to those around me, come neighbours, have good
    cheer,
The wheat again shall blossom and the barley grow for beer.
The lambkins they shall gambol down in the grassy glade,
The primrose buds shall open in the woodlands leafy shade,
And the poor heart-broken gardeners—I made them all so glad,
For I said that oft enthusiasts and the weather-wise were
    mad.

And the farmers came around me and fell each on bended knee,
And one held up a " tater," and 'tother held a pea ;
And they asked me should they plant them—I said, did *ever*
    Morgan lie ?

I tell you that the sunbeams again shall flush the sky :
I tell you that the Author shall ne'er disturb you more,
For he dreads the trip I'll give him to that hideous sterile
    shore—
So send ye out the sower, and fling abroad the grain,
For the earth shall burst with fatness when the Autumn
    comes again.

And they calmly hearken'd to me and sent their teams afield,
Although the meteorologist said lands would never yield—
Although he blindly stated that mighty rains would fall,
And that blighting frosts and mildew would be a deadly pall.
Although he grimly hinted that famine's ghost would come,
And that nature would be stricken, and her choristers be
    dumb ;
Yet the husbandman grew hopeful, and bared his strong right
    arm,
And smil'd at the Prophets' warning, which erst filled him
    with alarm.

And the whistle of the ploughman again was heard so shrill,
And soon the green blade budded, on mountain, mead, and hill,
And Flora flung her garlands, aye, broadcast o'er the land !
And the streamlets ran on laughing, toward the bright and
    golden sand : —
And men look'd up enraptured in wonder and surprise,
And thought upon the prophesy, and said—what awful lies !
Ne'er in man's living memory has there been a fairer spring,
Ne'er bloom'd there sweeter flowers—ne'er did sweeter
    music ring.

But friends, we must be grateful, and one and all should pray
That as the Author has no time to hope he never may,
So oft the same excuses—"it was for want of time"
His reckonings were erroneous, and I've been led to rhyme.
Had he, indeed, great leisure, we might see wonders strange ;
Perhaps the sun walk backwards, or the moon turn green for
    change—
Perhaps Nature's laws inverted—but my quill's worn to a
    stem,
So I just subscribe my compliments, and say—I'm C.D.M.

        ——

FAREWELL TO SUMMER.

      ——

  Farewell ; sweet time of mirth and flowers !
    Thou'rt fading fast away ;
  The gems which glittered o'er the earth
    Are trodden in the clay.
  The woods which thrilled with melody
    Are now all hushed and still ;
  And blighted are the heather bells
    Which bloomed on every hill.

  The leaflets stricken on the tree,
    Fall helpless, one by one,
  And e'en fair Nature's choristers
    Seem mourning Summer gone.

The swollen streamlet o'er its bed
   Sings now a sorrowing strain,—
For death is on the mountain-top,
   The moorland and the plain.

I watched the snowy hawthorn's bloom,
   The woodbine and the rose,
And, listening to the ring-dove's song,
   Forgotten were my woes.
But, like a fleeting fairy dream,
   The golden days are past,
And Autumn comes with chilling breath,
   And sadness in each blast.

'Twas in the stilly hours of night,
   When Nature seemed asleep,
That from the sterile Northern lands,
   A herald crossed the deep,—
'Twas but a whisper through the woods,—
   A voice across the plain—
But leaf and flow'ret knew their doom,
   And drooped as 'twere in pain—

A tremor seized the little birds
   That slumbered on the trees,
And sighing zephyrs died away,
   Before the angry breeze.
And when the cheering sunbeams came,
   How altered was the scene,
For sadness brooded o'er the place
   Where love and joy had been.

Then fare thee well, dear Summer time,
    Thy glorious reign is past;
Thou cloth'st the earth with loveliness
    Too fairy-like to last!
Thy mission o'er, thy work all done,
    Thou breath'st thy fond good-bye,
And paler glows the yellow sun
    Upon the low'ring sky,

Again farewell! 'tis hard to part,
    For dear art thou to me;
I love the jewels in thy lap,
    The green leaves on the tree;
I love the music thou dost bring—
    But now I hear thy knell!
And wildly, sadly could I weep,
    Sweet Summer, fare thee well!

WELCOME TO CHRISTMAS.

Hail! hoary old friend, thou art with us once more,
And the welcome we'll give thee shall surge round our shore,
For our song of rejoicing shall sweep o'er the plain,
As the right hand of friendship we give thee again.

Thou art with us indeed, and our hearts leap with glee,
And the holly and laurel thy green crown shall be,
And we'll hang up the mistletoe high over all,
For there's mirth in the cottage, the palace, and hall.

O we've waited thy coming, we've wished for thee long,
And we'll usher thee in with the dance and the song,
And we'll greet thee once more with the gladness of old,
For ere thy next advent what hearts may be cold!

There are places now vacant and loved ones "are not,"
There are hearts that are cheerless and loved ones forgot,
Ah! since thou wert here we have heard the death knell.
And the dark grave hath swallowed those cherished so well.

There are visions of fancy now shrouded in night,
There are souls that are writhing neath agony's blight,
There are wild hopes and longings that now must be vain,
For the dreamer hath 'wakened to sorrow and pain.

But away, with all sadness, black shadows must pass,
For time hath inverted the sands in life's glass,
So fill up the wine-cup and drain it, aye dry,
And dash down the tear-drop and banish the sigh.

For again there shall cluster around the bright fire,
The maid and her lover, the matron and sire,
And the sweet tales of childhood again shall be told,
As the grey-headed father forgets that he's old.

And mem'ry shall bear us away on her wing,
When our hearts were as bright as the rosebud in spring,
And we'll fling to the wild winds the fetters of care,
And mock at the spectre and laugh at despair.

Thrice hail! then old friend, thou art welcome once more,
And we'll greet thee again as we oft did of yore,
And our song of rejoicing shall sweep o'er the plain,
As the right hand of friendship we give thee again.

THE BROKEN BOUGH.

The wintry winds went shrieking through the trees,
And Vengeance rode upon the angered breeze —
And o'er the mountain and the blighted plain
Loud and still louder rose the cry of pain :
And morning's sunbeams, struggling o'er the sky,
Reveal'd strange wrecks and ruin to the eye ;
Dashed by the tempest to the soddened ground,
A broken bough, with ivy clad, I found.
Green was the ivy bud—the little spray
Had long fallen victim to a sad decay,—
And as I marked the living and the dead,
I thought a lesson might be truly read.
I saw that morning in the far back spring,
And heard the wild birds in the woodlands sing,
When first in fancy then it seemed to me,
The clasp of love encircled yon dead tree ;
And as the winters and the summers rolled,
Firmer and firmer grew each loving fold.
And there it clung, in savage storm and strife,
But ah ! it fed upon its lov'd ones' life—
Yet still how faithful, tho' the tree-top green
With smiling leaflets would no more be seen ;
No power could sever love's enduring tie,
They've lived together—they'll together die :
I bore away the little sapless bough,
To me each tendril seemed a deathless vow ;
Oh ! would that earthly love could be so pure,
Thro' time and trials ever to endure.

L

SUNRISE.

Hark! what are those sweet 'witching strains
That from the dewy vales arise ;
And what is that fair silvery streak
Which breaks along the eastern skies?

Again more loud the chorus swells,
The woodland warblers are awake ;
And onward sweeps the sweet refrain
From blushing tree-top, wood, and brake.

See, see it is the King of Day,
In all his glorious splendour drest ;
And proudly rolls old ocean's flood,
With dazzling sunbeams on its breast.

And high above the eastern hills,
Behold that world of lucid light ;
The moon and glittering stars grow pale,
And, trembling, hide away from sight.

The flow'rets heavenward turn and gaze,
As if fond praises they would sing ;
And then they fling their od'rous breath
To meet the zephyr's gentle wing.

The lambkins, startled from their sleep,
Bound o'er the daisied mead in play :
And myriad dewdrops fair as light
Hang pendant from each emerald spray.

And o'er the boundless azure sky
The rosy rainbow's flush steals on ;
And Nature laughs in rapt'rous glee
To know that darkness drear is gone.

THE WISH.

My wish is small, my aim it is not great :
Of gold, I'd say one hundred pounds a year ;
A cozy cottage—not a lordly seat—
On some fair hill-side let it stand, where trees
Shall wrestle stoutly with December's blasts,
Or make soft music in the Summer breeze.
Down in the vale let meadows green with flow'rs
    Be sprinkled o'er :
A tinkling brook I love, whose ripples kiss
The blue waves curling on the golden shore.
My garden small should overlook the vale,
And from my seat I'd view the smiling bay—
I love to watch the billows in their pride,
Or when they murmur, prance, and gleeful play.
Vain wish ! the world and I have quarrelled oft,
We've fought and I've been worsted—
    Dash'd on sorrows' road :
There scorn rode o'er me, crushed me in the dust,
Fell slander pierced me with its cruel goad,
Slander, that monster, prowls along our track,
Stabs, like a grim fiend, basely in the dark.
The suffering soul, when trouble settles deep,
Is slander's favor'd and its cherish'd mark ;
Its arrows, thick as those that fell

On Thermopylæ's Pass, and hid the sunlight
    From the Spartan's eye,
Have fallen on me—foul envy wing'd the dart,
    Malice took the aim,
And hatred drew the bow and bade them fly.
But I'll have another tussle with the world
In open light—with all its woes
I'll single-handed cope—
The baneful star that in my zenith rules,
Will to the Nadir soon revolve I hope,
And if I fail, what then? my old cap's brim
My spirit will not let me pull to stupid pride.
I court no favor from the haughty crew,
No, first may daisies my poor body hide!
The independent soul, "tho' clothed in rags,"
Though grief is round it more than can be told,
Looks with contempt upon those brainless ones
Whose only virtue is possessing gold.
Alone I've marched amid the warring world,
I seek no buoy to keep me on the wave;
Alone I'll battle with the billows fierce,
I'll cringe to none, to pity or to save.
And when to Mother Earth my dust returns,
And the green grass clusters tangles o'er my breast,
Perchance I'll sleep as sound as those great ones
Who 'neath their gaudy sculpt'red tablets rest.

Another wish I have, perhaps 'tis my last—
I'll ask it of some kind, some pitying friend:
To lay my body when my spirit's fled—

To lay me where the yew-tree's branches bend,
In some lone churchyard far from cities grand,
Far from all tumult and all ceaseless din :
I could not sleep where dreary walls are seen,
Amid the echo of a Babel's sin ;
I'd not find peace amid the mighty dead,
Not in that Abbey where earth's monarchs sleep ;
No, lay me where the suffering have found rest,
Where angels o'er the tortur'd victims weep.
Each mound around me let it be the bed
Of one who battled in life's darkest day ;
At midnight then the pitying spirits come,
And o'er the blighted sweetly sing and pray.
I want no mockery o'er my crumbling dust,
But in my mother's bosom, let me sleep—
The humblest flowres may bloom upon my bed,
When sunbeams thro' the waving branches creep.
'Tis all I ask, 'tis all, indeed, I crave,
A sanctuary from all griefs and care ;
The fulsome adulation on the chisel'd stone,
But taunts the mould'ring wreck that's rotting there !

RETROSPECTION.

There's a footpath through the woodlands
Which skirts the rippling rill,
Where I've wandered oft with Ellen,
When the village hum grew still;
In the springtide of my boyhood,
Ere pale sorrow lined my brow,
In that valley old I plighted
Love's fond and dearest vow.

And now it seems but yesterday
Tho' long weary years are past,
Since I breathed adieu to Ellen
As my heart throbbed wild and fast:
But all the fairy pictures,
Which our fond emotions drew,
Are vanished like frail shadows,
Tho' we deemed them real and true.

Yet mem'ry oft reminds me
Of our meeting in the dell,
On that sunny Summer evening
When I felt love's witching spell;
When with trembling hand I gathered
The violets—sweet and pale—
As I lisped my boyhood's passion,
And told my youthful tale.

ABSENCE.

Through ev'ry changing scene of life,
The trusting heart lives hoping on,
E'en when dark clouds obscure our path,
And every cheering ray is gone.

Tho' time rolls on and seas divide
Hearts bound in love's enduring chain ;
Yet still the heav'nly flame will burn
In tears and sorrow, woe and pain.

The envious world may sneer and frown,
The truest friend turn false and cold ;
But love that's pure may never change,
For love will shame e'en fire-tried gold.

PRINTED AT THE "CAMBRIAN" OFFICE, SWANSEA.